What Blood Can Do

AMY LAURENS

OTHER WORKS

SANCTUARY SERIES

Where Shadows Rise
Through Roads Between
When Worlds Collide

KADITEOS SERIES

How Not To Acquire A Castle

STORM FOXES SERIES

A Fox of Storms And Starlight

SHORTER WORKS AND COLLECTIONS

April Showers
Bones Of The Sea
Darkness And Good
Dreaming Of Forests
It All Changes Now
Of Sea Foam And Blood
Rush Job
The Ice Cream Crown Skating Races
Trust Issues

NON-FICTION

How To Plan A Pinterest-Worthy Party Without Dying
How To Write Dogs
How To Theme
How To Create Cultures
How To Create Life
How To Map
The 32 Worst Mistakes People Make About Dogs

Find other works by the author at www.amylaurens.com

What Blood Can Do

INKLET #82

AMY LAURENS

Inkprint
PRESS
www.inkprintpress.com

Print ISBN: 978-1-922434-22-7
eBook ISBN: 9798201636968

www.inkprintpress.com

National Library of Australia Cataloguing-in-Publication Data
Laurens, Amy 1985 –
What Blood Can Do
30 p.
ISBN: 978-1-922434-22-7
Inkprint Press, Canberra, Australia
1. Young Adult Fiction—Fantasy—Dark Fantasy 2. Young Adult Fiction—Fantasy—Contemporary 3. Young Adult Fiction—Family—Parents 4. Young Adult Fiction—Short Stories, Collections & Anthologies

First Print Edition: May 2022
Cover photo © Enrique Meseguer via Pixabay
Cover design © Inkprint Press
Interior art © Amy Laurens

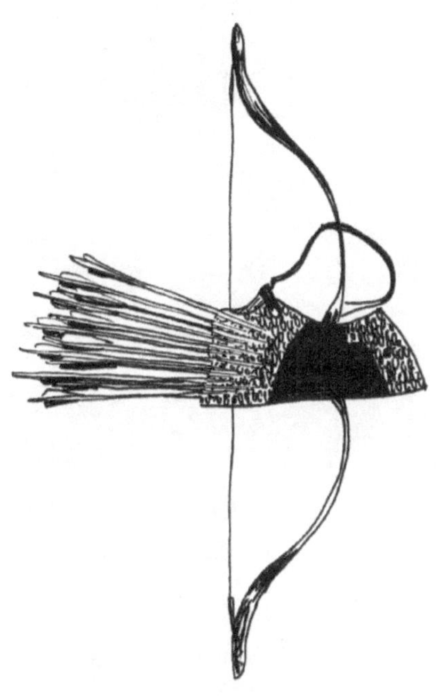

WHAT BLOOD CAN DO

Eıght years ago, my father slaugh-
tered my mother. He tied her down on
the dining table with guy ropes and slit
her throat with the bread knife. It
wasn't sharp. There was so much
blood I thought it would never stop.

I screamed.

I thought I'd never stop.

My father left me there, ten years
old and elbow deep in the pulsing river
of my mother's life. He told me he was
sorry. My fingers burned to use the

knife on him. With blood tingling over my skin, I swore I'd have my revenge.

I called the cops, of course; I was ten, not stupid. I told them what I'd seen, and they bounced me along the foster-care chain after booking me appointments with Phyllis. She gave me lollipops and sympathetic glances over her gold-wired glasses. It didn't help. I had to see her, though, until at last I promised I was starting to heal.

I lied.

When I was fourteen, we did archery for sport at school. I loved it: it was soothing, focused—and practical. I sliced my finger on an arrow that first time, testing to see if it could kill a man. The blood got all over my bow-string.

I never missed a shot.

I joined the local archery club, working clean-up in their café to pay the fees. I practiced every day, without fail.

At sixteen, I was winning state tournaments.

At seventeen, I won the nationals.

At eighteen, it was time to hunt him down.

On impulse, I sat down with a phone book. As I opened it, one page papercut my thumb and blood smeared across it. I hissed sharply, but dialled the bloodied number.

It was him; I'd know his voice beyond the grave.

He agreed to meet me at the Okahawa Trail, too eager for anything that smacked of reconciliation to have a sense of self-preservation.

I shot him.

It would have been a good, clean kill too, right in the throat—a nice sense of irony, I thought—but the arrow had been knocked a little off course by a freak gust of wind.

I could have walked away, left him to die. The bolt was only a standard cut-on-contact broadhead; any local deer hunter would have used the same. But since he was going to be alive for another minute, I figured he might as well know why I'd done it.

I didn't expect the tears. My own, I mean; I assume it's pretty normal for your eyes to fill with liquid when you've had your throat pierced and are about to die. But as I stood over him, desperately bricking up the wall around my feelings, tears welled up and overflowed. "You bastard," I whispered. "Why did you kill her?"

He stared up at me with eyes wide—fear, pain, guilt, who could tell?—gasping and gurgling as the blood oozed away.

My stomach knotted as I remembered: a bread knife, ropes tied to the dining table, my forearms tingling, up to my elbows in my mother's blood. Disgusted, I turned away.

"Wait," he rasped. "Stop."

I stopped, but didn't turn around.

"She... was trying... kill you."

I whirled on him. "How dare you. How *dare* you! You, you *murderer*!" I spat.

"Blood," he wheezed. "Her blood."

"Yes," I said, locking him in a steely glare. "There was a lot of blood. I should know; you abandoned me in it."

"Not... abandoned. Saved."

I snorted and stalked off.

"Cassie. Your blood. You never miss."

I froze. "How do you know that?" How could he possibly know the reason why the club members called me Zero? How did he know I'd never missed a shot?

"She... same. You get... from her."

I inched back around to face him, heart exploding in my chest. "What are you saying?"

"She... Your mother... Fae."

The rough trunk of a tree caught me as I lurched.

"The blood... you have her blood."

My mind whirled as I remembered every incident I'd passed off as co-incidence, all those times I'd thought I'd just been lucky. Every time, the blood. "Why did you kill her?" I whispered.

"She would have killed you. The Blood"—I heard the capital letter this time—"calls to blood. Any... any daughter of hers... competition."

I sank to the ground beside my father. The ooze of red at his neck was coming thicker now.

Desperation surged. I snatched at my sweater, tearing ineffectually before stripping it off to press against his wound. "She wanted to kill me?" I said, still whispering. This time, it wasn't the memories of luck that came, but of unluck: of all the times I'd nearly died before I was ten. The time I fell in the gap between the train and the platform; the time I fell from a second-storey balcony and rolled down concrete steps. My grandparents used to joke that I was made of rubber, that I was the most accident-prone child they'd ever seen.

I didn't have a single accident after I was ten.

"It wasn't... her fault," he said through the gasps. "The Blood. You have her power. It... drove her crazy. Blood... never share its power."

My father's blood seeped through my sweater and stickied my fingers. I stared at the red-streaked whorls of my left-hand fingerprints. Was it true?

I snatched another arrow from my quiver and sliced the tip across my palm. I let the blood well for a moment. A tingling sensation covered the palm of my hand, familiar and comforting—and unright. It wasn't the feeling of injury, but something more; my lifeblood pulsing with energy—and power.

The truth crushed me, robbing my lungs of air. My mother had tried to kill me, more times than I could remember.

My father had killed her to save me.

And I'd come here for revenge.

I stared as the blood of the one who'd murdered to save me ebbed away. "I'm sorry," I whispered. "I'm so sorry."

He didn't answer, his face grey and clammy.

I hated him for killing my mother, even if she had been trying to kill me; I hated him for making me what I'd become, for not telling me, for not trusting me.

But I couldn't hate him if he was dead.

I pressed my wounded palm against his neck. My blood had been keeping me safe for eighteen years.

Time to find out what it could really do.

THE MAKING OF
WHAT BLOOD CAN DO

This story was an exercise in practising flash fiction (stories shorter than a thousand words). I had no real plan when I began it other than to explore the consequences of a) misconstrued actions and b) a child witnessing the death of someone they loved.

Perhaps this was catalysed by looking back at my own childhood with new eyes; it's interesting how, when we really look, adult hindsight can lend new meaning to events of our childhood in ways that dramatically shift our approach to life—and the world.

And, of course, to the people involved in those past events.

Read more by Amy Laurens!

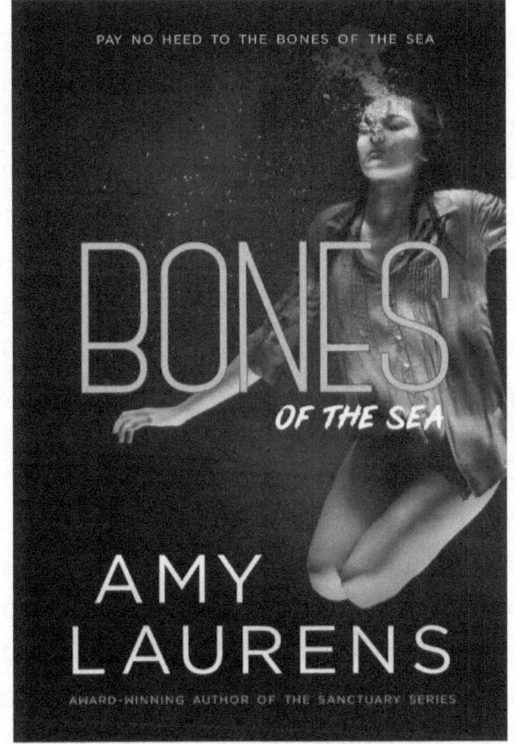

BONES OF THE SEA

THE MAN—WHOSE NAME IS IRRELEVANT, FOR HE shall soon be dead—wandered down the beach where sand whiter than any he'd seen before swashed between a short, head-high cliff to his left, and the frothing waves of the ocean to his right. Salt filled the air, but below that, something else lingered, and he couldn't quite place his… nose… on what it was.

Of course, the locals were horrified that he was here at all. But he was a Man Of Learning, and was not accustomed to heeding the warnings of people obviously less learned than himself, especially when they spoke tales of a beach that left no trespasser alive.

He'd scoffed. Ridiculous, their legends of a beach where to set one toe on the sand was to seal your own death sentence before the rising of the next full moon.

He was far more interested in ana-lysing the sand, quite literally whiter than any he'd seen before, and thus far resistant to his attempts to decode it. He'd thought a pure variety of quartz before he'd arrived, but upon reaching the beach, pulling into the little de-serted cul-de-sac dead end festooned with warning signs ('Cursed Beach, Do Not Enter'; 'Beware The Bones Of The Sea'), he'd switched his engine off, opened the car door to the sound of waves and wind through the saltbush, and he'd seen the sharp drop-off down to the sand and had changed his mind to chalk, or maybe gypsum.

But there'd been no tiny fossils his portable microscope could detect, and the sand, whatever it was made from, had failed to fizz under the application of a drop of acid from his little glass vial, so that struck gypsum and chalk from the list of options.

Now, after several hours on the beach to no avail as the hot evening sun seared his hands and the light glinting off both ocean and white sand blinded him, he'd had enough. He'd run out of fresh water, ideas, and patience all, and was presently hiking back around the cove to his car that glinted silver and tantalising at the far end of the beach, a haven of cool air and fresh water.

Stay. Stay a little while longer.

The salt clung to his skin, filming his lips, the inside of his nose, the back of his throat. Somehow, the ocean smelled sharper here, more concentrated. Briefly, he wondered if that was the source of the townsfolk's rumours; but a higher salt concentration ought to have meant people floated better, drowned less. No. There must simply be a convergence of factors that meant the currents here were particularly treacherous, and indeed, casting his gaze out to the distant horizon, examining the interplay of wave and off-white foam, the cove did seem to be quite swirly, with a few smooth tracts he thought were probably rips.

As ever, folklore had a logical series of explanations behind it.

Just a little longer.

His leather sandal caught on something in the sand.

He stumbled.

Ow. That hurt.

Whatever it was, it had poked through the holes in his footwear to stab at his toes.

Glaring, impatient, our nameless victim kicked away some of the strange, defiant white sand—and inhaled sharply.

Once the initial burst of adrenalin subsided—something a surprise human skull will inevitably inspire, regardless of one's general composure—it seemed obvious.

Of course. The one thing he hadn't tested for was bone.

So focused on unlocking the mystery of the sand's composition was he that his initial reaction was deep, gleeful satisfaction.

Dawning understanding, however, made him lift his feet, hesitantly at first, shaking the white sand—bone—sand, think of it as sand, it's safer that way—but it's bone, really it's bone, it's all bone, every single grain of it, pure white, sun-bleached bone, spat up from the guts of the ocean the way a predatory owl spits out the bones of its prey—and then his feet were dancing, just like his stomach, as he leapt for the cliff and tried to haul himself up and off the beach because God, oh God, he was standing on bones and only bones, and the skull he'd uncovered had been human, and there, just down the beach, that rock wasn't a rock, it was another skull, and oh God, how many people had died here?

He realised the sobbing was his, rasps of panic as he scrabbled at the embankment that should have been easier to climb than it was, his fingers digging at the rock, skin tearing, sandals scraping for purchase…

Stay.

His back was to the ocean when the freak wave rose, a local tsunami of salt and hunger.

It smashed into him.

As it dragged him out to sea, all he felt was cold, so bitter it froze his bones right in his body.

An hour later, as the sun spilled red-orange lifeblood out over the ocean, the ocean spat a skull, bleached-white and grinning, back up onto the beach. A moment later, as the full moon crested over the craggy headland behind, a sternum—*most* of its ribs still attached—joined the skull, followed a moment later by a single scapula.

And as the moon rose and the ocean swallowed the sun, a whisper began that sounded like the wind… until you realised there was nothing but salt-bush for the wind to disturb, and the whispers sounded strangely like a voice, hungry, crooning, and singing.

Feed me.

Feeed mee.

Feeeed meeeeee….

Keep reading! Head to www.inkprintpress.com/amylaurens/bonesofthesea/ to buy your copy now!

ABOUT THE AUTHOR

AMY LAURENS is an Australian author of fantasy fiction for all ages. Although she does not have magic blood, she definitely does love archery.

Amy has also written the award-winning portal-fantasy *Sanctuary* series about Edge, a 13-year-old girl forced to move to a small country town because of witness protection (the first book is *Where Shadows Rise*), the humorous fantasy *Kaditeos* series, following newly graduated Evil Overlord Mercury as she attempts to acquire a castle, the young adult series *Storm Foxes*, about love and magic and family in small town Australia, and a whole host of non-fiction and shorter works.

INKLETS

Collect them all! Released on the 1st and 15th
of each month.

INKLET #088
Some
Impropriety
Expected
AMY LAURENS

INKLET #089
NEON SNOW
LIANA BROOKS

INKLET #090
Reincarnation
LIANA BROOKS

INKLET #091
More Than
Mushrooms
AMY LAURENS

DOUBLE ISSUE
INKLET #092
How To Make A Star
& The World Ended
LIANA BROOKS

INKLET #093
CAUGHT
IN THE ACT
AMY LAURENS

INKLET #094
ANUBIS
Has Sent You
Six Souls
LIANA BROOKS

INKLET #095
PRAYER TO A
GODDESS
LIANA BROOKS

INKLET #096
Love In The
Time Of Corona
AMY LAURENS

www.ingramcontent.com/pod-product-compliance
Lightning Source LLC
Chambersburg PA
CBHW062003190726
48285CB00003BA/1177